HANDA'S NOISY NIGHT

EILEEN BROWNE

WALKER BOOKS
AND SUBSIDIARIES

LONDON • BOSTON • SYDNEY • AUCKLAND

Handa came to stay the night
with her friend, Akeyo.

"Mum says we can sleep in the hut," said Akeyo.

"That will be fun!" said Handa.

"Goodnight," said Akeyo's mum and dad.

"Sleep tight," said her nan and grandad.

The girls took sweetcorn and toys to the hut.

Handa was really excited.

"I can hear snorting!" said Handa.

"It's Dad," said Akeyo.

"He snorts when he laughs."

"What's that chattering?" said Handa.

"Just the grown-ups," said Akeyo.

"Talking and talking."

chatter
chatter

"Now there's rattling!" said Handa.

"Don't worry," said Akeyo.

"It's Mum, playing the shaker."

rattle

rattle

"Something's squeaking!" said Handa.

"That's Grandad," said Akeyo.

"Wheeling his rusty old bike."

"Can you hear slurping?" said Handa.

"Yes." Akeyo yawned.

"Nan's drinking her bedtime milk."

"Oh no – someone's crying!" said Handa.

"Only my … baby sister,"

said Akeyo, falling asleep.

Thud!

"What's that?" Handa held her breath.

"Maybe it's … a door slamming."

She closed her eyes. "Night night, Akeyo."

Next morning, Handa woke to a *tap-tap-tapping*.

"Someone's at the door," said Akeyo. "Come in!"

"That's funny," said Handa. "There's no one here."

"Hello!" said Akeyo's mum. "Did you sleep well?"

"Not really," said Akeyo.

"You were all too noisy!"

"We were quiet as mice," said the grown-ups.

"Oh!" said Handa.

"So *who* was making the noise?"

woodpecker

owl

pig

porcupine

pangolin

fox

bush-baby

bat